The Go-Kart Race

Adapted by John Dougherty

Every day, the Kingdom of Sugar Rush held a go-kart race. To enter, the kart drivers put a gold coin into King Candy's special pot. All the coins were given to the winner.

Vanellope just *knew* that, given the chance, she could win.

The problem was she didn't have a coin to pay her race fee, or a kart to drive.

Then one day, Vanellope met Wreck-It Ralph climbing a peppermint tree. At the top of the tree, something was gleaming.

"A gold coin!" she yelled excitedly, and scrambled up the tree to grab it.

"It's my medal!" shouted Ralph.

Vanellope raced off with Ralph's medal, and put it in King Candy's pot. Her name appeared on the list of racers. She was in!

As for the kart ... "Here it is – the Lickety-Split!" she said proudly. "Built it myself!"

The other racers weren't impressed and she was chased from the race.

"You have to back out," Taffyta told her. "King Candy says you can't race. You're an accident just waiting to happen."

Taffyta tore the little kart's steering wheel off and threw it away.

Taffyta's friends surrounded the kart and began to destroy it. "You'll never be a racer!" Taffyta sneered.

"What are you doing?" Vanellope yelped. "Please! I just want to race like you guys!"

Luckily for Vanellope, Wreck-It Ralph had been looking for her, and was watching from a hiding place.

Ralph did not like bullies.

"Hey! Leave her alone!" he roared, charging at them.

Taffyta and her friends shrieked, and jumped into their karts.

"Scram!" Ralph shouted, as they raced away.

Vanellope was saved – but her kart was ruined.

Ralph was still angry with Vanellope about the medal, but Vanellope had an idea.

"You help me get a new kart," she said. "Then I'll win the race and get you back your medal. What do you say, friend?"

"You better win!" said Ralph grumpily, and they shook hands to agree on the plan.

Everything in Sugar Rush was made of sweets, cakes or biscuits – even the go-karts. So Ralph and Vanellope sneaked into the kart bakery.

"Where are the karts?" asked Ralph.

"We gotta make one!" Vanellope told him.

Wreck-It Ralph thought this was a bad idea. Breaking things was his only skill.

However, Vanellope needed his help, so he tried his best. Together they baked a kart for the race.

The kart didn't look very good.

"I tried to warn you," said Ralph.
"I can't make things. I just break things."

"I love it!" Vanellope squealed in excitement.
"I finally have a real kart!"

As she was admiring the kart, the door opened, and a voice said, "Hold it right there!"

It was King Candy, and with him were his Doughnut Police!

"Get that girl!" he cried. "Destroy that kart. She can't be allowed to race!"

Quickly, Ralph picked Vanellope up and plonked her in the driver's seat.

"Start the kart!" he said urgently, hopping on behind her. "What are you waiting for? Let's go!"

"I don't know how to drive a real kart!" Vanellope confessed, embarrassed.

There was only one thing for it. Ralph reached down and pushed as hard as he could, propelling the kart forward. It shot out of the bakery and away.

"Stop in the name of the King!" King Candy shouted. He jumped into his own kart and chased after them.

With Wreck-It Ralph's extra power, Vanellope's kart was too fast for King Candy. They left him behind …

... and reached Vanellope's secret hideout.

Now all Ralph had to do was teach Vanellope to drive, and then maybe she could get his medal back!